KB084045

갯마을

아시아에서는 《바이링궐 에디션 한국 대표 소설》을 기획하여 한국의 우수한 문학을 주제별로 엄선해 국내외 독자들에게 소개합니다. 이 기획은 국내외 우수한 번역가들이 참여하여 원작의 품격을 최대한 살렸습니다. 문학을 통해 아시아의 정체성과 가치를 살피는 데 주력해 온 아시아는 한국인의 삶을 넓고 깊게 이해하는 데 이 기획이 기여하기를 기대합니다.

Asia Publishers presents some of the very best modern Korean litera-ture to readers worldwide through its new Korean literature series 〈Bi-lingual Edition Modern Korean Literature〉. We are proud and happy to offer it in the most authoritative translation by renowned translators of Korean literature. We hope that this series helps to build solid bridges between citizens of the world and Koreans through a rich in-depth understanding of Korea.

바이링궐 에디션 한국 대표 소설 100

Bi-lingual Edition Modern Korean Literature 100

Seaside Village

오영수
갯마을

Oh Yeongsu

ASIA
PUBLISHERS

Contents

갯마을

Seaside Village

서(西)로 멀리 기차 소리를 바람결에 들으며, 어쩌면 동해 파도가 돌각담 밑을 찰싹대는 H라는 조그만 갯마을이 있다.

더께더께 굴딱지가 붙은 모 없는 돌로 담을 쌓고, 낡은 삿갓 모양 옹기종기 엎딘 초가가 스무 집 될까 말까? 조그마한 멸치 후리막[1]이 있고, 미역으로 이름이 있으나, 이 마을 사내들은 대부분 철 따라 원양출어(遠洋出漁)에 품팔이를 나간다. 고기잡이 아낙네들은 썰물이면 조개나 해조를 캐고, 밀물이면 채마밭이나 매는 것으로 여느 갯마을이나 별다름 없다. 다르다고 하면 이 마을에는 유독 과부가 많은 것이라고나 할까? 고로(古老)들

There is a small seaside village where the sound of a distant train can be heard on the west wind and where the waves of the East Sea slap from time to time at the base of a wall of piled rocks.

The walls inside the village are built of large, round boulders, encrusted with layers of mussel shells; and the grass-roofed cottages, huddled together like so many old straw rain hats probably number around twenty. The village has a small tower for sitting in to watch for anchovies and it is known for its edible seaweed. Most of the able-bodied young men, however, are hired to work in deep-sea fishing depending on the season. The

은 과부가 많은 탓을 뒷산이 어떻게 갈라져서 어찌어찌 돼서 그렇다느니, 앞바다 물발이 거세서 그렇다느니들 했고, 또 모두 그렇게들 믿고 있다.

해순이도 과부였다. 과부들 중에서도 가장 젊은 스물셋의 청상이었다.

초여름이었다. 어느 날 밤, 조금 떨어진 멸치 후리막에서 꽹과리 소리가 들려왔다. 여름 들어 첫 꽹과리다. 마을은 갑자기 수선대기 시작했다. 멸치 떼가 몰려온 것이다. 멸치 떼가 들면 막에서는 꽹과리나 나팔로 신호를 한다. 그러면 마을 사람들은 막으로 달려가서 그물을 당긴다. 그물이 올라 수확이 많으면 많은 대로 적으면 적은 대로 '짓'이라고 해서 대개는 잡어(雜魚)를 나눠 받는다. 수고의 대가다. 그렇기 때문에 후리를 당기러 갈 때는 광주리나 바구니를 결코 잊지 않았고 대부분이 아낙네들이다. 갯마을의 가장 풍성하고 즐거운 때다. 해순이도 부지런히 헌옷을 갈아입고 나갈 차비를 하는데, 담 밖에서 숙이 엄마가 숨찬 소리로,

"새댁 안 가?"

"같이 가요, 잠깐……."

"다들 갔다, 빨리 나오잖고……."

wives of the fishermen collect clams and seaweed at low tide and tend their vegetable gardens when the tide is in. In all, it is no different from any other seaside village. If one were to speak of a difference, perhaps it would be that this village in particular has quite a few widows. The old men blame the number of widows on the shape and arrangement of the mountains inland or on the roughness of the coastal tidal currents. Everyone believes that this is true.

Haesun was a widow. At twenty-three, she was the youngest of all the widows in the village.

It was early summer. One evening the sound of a gong was heard from the anchovy watch-tower, which stood by the water a short distance from the village. It was the first gong since summer had begun. The village suddenly stirred to life. A school of anchovies had gathered.

Whenever a school of anchovies approached, someone would signal from the watch-tower with a gong or a trumpet. When the villagers heard it, they would run towards the watch-tower to grab hold of the net. When the net emerged from the water, the odd fish in the catch would be divided as a bonus among those who had helped—more or

"아따, 빨리 가면 짓 먼첨 받나 머!"

하고 해순이가 사립 밖을 나서자, 숙이 엄마는,

"아이구 요것아!"

눈앞에 대고 헛주먹질을 하면서,

"맴(홑)치마만 걸치면 될 걸…… 꼬물대고서……."

"망측하게 또 맴치마다. 성님(형님)은 정말 맴치마래?"

"밤인데 누가 보나 머, 철벙대고 적시노면 빨기 구찮고……."

사실 그물 당기고 보면 으레 옷이 젖는다. 식수도 간신히 나눠먹는 갯마을이라 빨래가 여간 아니다. 그래서 아낙네들은 맨발에 홑치마만 두르고 나오는 버릇이 생겼는지도 모른다. 그로 해서 또 젊은 사내들의 짓궂은 장난도 있다. 어쩌면 사내들의 짓궂은 장난을 싫찮게 받아들이는 갯마을 여인들인지도 모른다.

해순이와 숙이 엄마는 물기슭 모래톱으로 해서 후리막으로 달려갔다. 맨발에 추진 모래가 한결 시원하다. 벌써 후리는 시작되었다. 굵직한 로프 줄에는 후리꾼들이 지네발처럼 매달렸다.

—데에야 데야.

이켠과 저켠에서 이렇게 서로 주고받으면 로프는 팽

less, depending upon the size of the haul. It was the price of their toil. For this reason, no one ever forgot to bring along a basket or hamper, and most of the workers were women. It was the most happy and prosperous season in the life of this seaside village.

Haesun was busily changing into old clothes and getting ready to go when Sugi's mother called to her breathlessly over the wall.

"Aren't you going, Haesun?"

"Let's go together. Just a moment."

"Everyone else has already gone! If you don't come quickly..."

"Oh, lord! Are the first ones there the first to get the bonus?"

As Haesun emerged from her brushwood gate, Sugi's mother saw her clothes and waved a finger in her face.

"Oh, my. What a trial you are! When all you have to do is throw on just a skirt. Such dawdling!"

"No! Just a skirt? Really, sister? Is that all you're wearing?"

"It's night—who can see? Anyway, it's a bother to wash all that clothing after you splash into the water and get soaked."

팽해지면서 지그시 당겨온다. 해순이와 숙이 엄마도 아무렇게나 빈틈에 끼여들어 줄을 잡았다. 바다 저만치서 선두가 칸델라 불을 흔들고 고함을 지른다.

당겨 올린 줄을 뒷거둠질하는 사내들이, 데에야 데야를 선창해서 후리꾼들의 기세를 돋우고, 막 거간들이 바쁘게들 서성댄다. 가마솥에는 불이 활활 타고 물이 끓는다. 그물이 가까워 올수록 이 데에야 데야는 박자가 빨라진다.

—데야 데야 데야 데야.

이때쯤은 벌써 멸치가 모래톱에 헤뜩헤뜩 뛰어오른다. 멸치가 많이 들면 수면이 부풀어 오르고 그물주머니가 터지는 때도 있다. 이날 밤도 멸치는 무던히 든 모양이다. 선두는 곧장 칸델라를 흔든다. 후리꾼들도 신이 난다.

—데야 데야 데야 데야.

이때 해순이 손등을 덮어 쥐는 억센 손이 있었다. 줄과 함께 검잡힌 손은 해순이 힘으로는 어쩔 수 없었다. 내버려두었다. 후리꾼들의 호흡은 더욱 거칠고 빨라진다. 억센 손은 어느새 해순이의 허리를 감싸 안는다. 해순이는 그만 줄 밑으로 빠져 나와 딴 자리로 옮아버린

When the net was pulled in, their clothing usually got wet. In a seaside village with barely enough water for drinking, laundry was no easy matter. This was probably why the women customarily pulled in the nets barefoot and wearing only their outer skirts. The young men used this opportunity to play annoying tricks. And the village women, for their part, may well not have disliked the pranks of their young men.

Haesun and Sugi's mother raced along the beach at the water's edge towards the watch-tower. The wet sand felt cool beneath their bare feet. The others had already begun to bring in the net. The pullers seemed to dangle from the heavy rope like the legs from a centipede.

Te-e-ya, te-ya!

The rope tightened to their steady pulling as the group at one end of the net echoed the chorus of the group at the other end. Haesun and Sugi's mother slipped into what openings they could find and grabbed onto the rope. Shouts could be heard from the small boat out on the water where signal lanterns were moving. The young men hauled on the rope as they moved backwards, raising a chorus to urge on the net-handlers: *te-e-ya, te-ya!* At

다. 그물도 거진 올라왔다.

—야세 야세.

이때는 사내들이 물기슭으로 뛰어들어 그물주머니를 한곳으로 모아드는 판이다. 누가 또 해순이 치마 밑으로 손을 디민다. 해순이는 반사적으로 획 뿌리치고 저만치 달아나 버린다. 멸치가 모래 위에 하얗게 뛴다. 아낙네들은 뛰어오른 멸치들을 주워 담기에 바쁘다. 후리는 끝났다. 멸치는 큰 그물 쪽자로 광주리에 퍼서 다시 돌(시멘트)함에 옮겨 잡어를 골라낸다. 이래서 멸치가 굵으면 젓감으로 날로 넘기기도 하고, 잘면 삶아서 이리꼬[2)]를 만든다.

해순이는 짓을 한 바구니 받았다. 무겁도록 이고 아낙네들과 함께 돌아오면서도 괜히 가슴이 설렌다. 짓보다는 그 억센 손이 머릿속을 떠나지 않는다. 누굴까? 유독 짓을 많이 주던 막 거간이나 아니던가? 누가 엿보지나 않았을까? 망측해라!

해순이는 유독 짓이 많은 것이 아낙네들 보기에 무슨 죄나 지은 것처럼 부끄럽기만 했다. 그래서 해순이는 되도록 뒤처져 가기로 발을 멈추자, 숙이 엄마가 옆구리를 쿡 찌르면서,

the watch-tower, the fish-brokers bustled. Flames lapped at the iron caldron where water boiled. As the net drew closer to the shore, the beat of the chant quickened.

Te-ya, te-ya, te-ya, te-ya!

By this time, the anchovies were already churning up white water in the shallows. There were times, indeed, when so many anchovies were trapped that the surface of the water boiled up and the pocket of the net would burst. It looked like quite a few anchovies had been caught this night. Signal lanterns continued to wave from the bow of the boat. The net-handlers worked with mounting excitement.

Te-ya, te-ya, te-ya, te-ya!

At this moment, Haesun felt a strong hand close over hers. With her hand held against the rope, Haesun was not strong enough to do anything about it. She released the rope for a moment. The panting of the net-handlers grew even more violent and fast. The strong hand then grasped Haesun's waist but she ducked under the rope and slipped away to another spot. The net was almost landed by now.

Ya-se, ya-se!

"너 운 짓이 그렇게도 많에?"

해순이는 얼른 뭐라고 대답이 나오지 않았다. 주니까 받아왔을 뿐이다.

"흥 알아봐서, 요 깍쟁이……."

아낙네들이 모두 킥킥대고 웃는다. 뭔지 까닭 있는 웃음들이다. 짐작이 있는 웃음들인지도 모른다. 해순이는 귀밑이 화앗 달았다. 숙이 엄마네 집 앞에서 해순이는,

"성님, 내 짓 좀 줄까?"

숙이 엄마는,

"준 사람에게 뺨 맞게……."

그러면서도 바구니를 내민다. 해순이는 짓을 반이 넘게 부어주었다.

해순이는 아랫도리를 헹구고 들어와서 자리에 누웠으나 오래도록 잠이 오질 않는다. 그 억센 손이 자꾸만 머릿속에 떠오른다. 돌아오지 않는, 어쩌면 꼭 돌아올 것도 같은 성구(聖九)의 손 같기도 한, 아니면 또 징용으로 끌려가버린 상수의 손 같기도 한─그 억세디억센 손…….

해순이는 생각을 떨쳐 버리려고 애써본다. 눈을 감아 잠을 청해 본다. 그러나 금하는 음식일수록 맘이 당기

Some of the men had gathered at the water's edge and were closing off the pocket of the net. Then someone slipped his hand up under Haesun's skirt. Haesun instinctively shook herself loose and dashed away. The anchovies danced white on the sand. The women were busily gathering the dancing anchovies. The netting was over. With pieces of net, they scooped the anchovies into round, wicker baskets and then transferred them to a large cement basin. The odd fish were divided up among those who had helped. The large anchovies were set aside, uncooked, for later pickling and the smaller ones were boiled on the spot for later drying.

As her bonus, Haesun received a basketful of fish so heavy she had to carry it on her head. Her breast was trembling while she returned with the other women. Rather than thinking of the bonus, her mind was filled with thoughts of that strong hand. Whose could it have been? The broker at the watch-tower who gave her such a large bonus? Could someone have noticed them? How dreadful!

Having received so large a bonus, Haesun felt guilty in front of the other women, as if she had committed some crime. But as she paused in an ef-

듯 잊어버리려고 애를 쓰면 쓸수록 놓치기 싫은 마음—
그것은 해순이에게 까마득 사라져가는 기억의 불씨를
솟구쳐 사르개[3]를 지펴놓은 것과도 같았다. 안타깝고
괴로운 밤이었다.

창이 밝아왔다. 해순이는 방문을 열었다. 사리섬 위에
달이 솟았다. 해순이는 달빛에 산산조각으로 부서진 바
다를 바라보면서 이렇게 뇌어본다.

—죽었는지 살았는지.

눈시울이 젖는다. 한숨과 함께 혀를 한번 차고는 문지
방을 베고 누워 버린다. 달빛에 젖어 잠이 들었다.

누가 어깨를 흔든다. 소스라치고 깨어보니 그의 시어
머니다. 해순이는 벌떡 일어나 가슴을 여미면서,

"우짜고, 그새 잠이 들었던가베……."

시어머니는 언제나 다름없는 부드럽고 낮은 소리로,

"얘야, 문을 닫아걸고 자거라!"

남편 없는 며느리가 애처로웠고, 아들 없는 시어머니
가 가엾어 친딸 친어머니 못지않게 정으로 살아가는 고
부간이다. 그러나 이날 밤만은 얼굴이 달아올라 해순이
는 고개를 들 수가 없었다. 그의 시어머니는 언젠가 해
순이가 되돌아오기 전에도,

fort to fall as far behind the others as possible, Sugi's mother poked her in the ribs.

"How come you got such a big bonus?"

Haesun had no ready answer. She had simply taken what she had been given.

"Ah, I've got it! You're a clever one!"

The women all giggled merrily. There was a reason behind their laughter. It seemed a knowing laughter to her. Haesun felt a hot flush creep up behind her ears. They were in front of Sugi's mother's house.

"Sister, shall I give you some of my bonus?"

"What? And get slapped by the man who gave it to you?" she said, proffering her basket at the same time. Haesun gave her more than half her bonus.

Haesun rinsed off her legs and went in to lie down but she was unable to sleep. Over and over the thought of that strong hand invaded her reveries. A hand like Songgu's, who had never come back, though it had seemed so sure he would; or a hand like Sangsu's, who had been taken away forever by the army—a strong, compelling hand.

Haesun tried hard to put away these thoughts. Closing her eyes, she prayed for sleep. Just as forbidden fruit becomes attractive, the more she strove to put these feelings out of her mind, the

"얘야, 문을 꼭 걸고 자거라!"

고 한 적이 있었다. 그날 밤의 기억이 너무나 생생하게 떠올랐기 때문이었다. 모든 것을 다 알고 있는 그의 시어머니다. 어쩌면 해순이의 오늘은 이 '얘야, 문을 꼭 닫아걸고 자거라……'는 데 요약될는지도 모른다.

해순이는 보재기[海女]딸이다. 그의 어머니가 김가라는 뜨내기 고기잡이 애를 배자 이 마을을 떠나지 못했다. 그래서 해순이가 났다. 해순이는 그의 어머니를 따라 바위 그늘과 모래밭에서 바닷바람에 그슬리고 조개껍질을 만지작거리고 갯냄새에 절어서 컸다. 열 살 때부터는 잠수도 배웠다. 해순이가 성구에게로 시집을 가기는 열아홉 살 때였다. 해순이의 성례⁴⁾를 보자 그의 어머니는 그의 고향인 제주도로 가면서,

"너 땜에 이십 년 동안 고향 땅을 못 밟았다. 인제는 마음 놓고 간다. 너도 인젠 가장을 섬기는 몸이니 아예 에미 생각을랑 마라……."

고깃배에 실려 그의 어머니는 물길로 떠났다.

해순이에게 장가들기가 소원이던 성구는 그만치 해순이를 아꼈다. 성구는 해순이에게 물일도 시키지 않았

more she was loath to forsake them. Haesun felt the embers of a fading memory stir into flame. It was a night of frustration and pain.

When the window grew light, Haesun opened the door to her room. The moon had risen over Sari Island. As she looked out on the surface of the ocean, which shattered the reflected light of the moon, she repeated over and over, *Has he died or does he live?*

Her eyes brimmed with tears. She sighed and tutted and then, pillowing her head on the threshold, stretched out. Drenched in moonlight, Haesun finally fell asleep.

Someone was shaking her shoulder. She awoke with a start to find it was her mother-in-law. Haesun leapt up, straightening her blouse.

"I must have fallen asleep!"

The mother-in-law responded in the quiet and gentle tone she always used.

"Come now, child. You must lock your door before you go to sleep."

These two sorry women—the one without her son and the other without her husband—lived together as closely as a real mother and daughter. But on this particular night Haesun could not lift her reddened

다. 워낙 착실한 성구라 제 혼자 힘만으로도 넉넉지는
못하나마 그의 홀어머니와 동생 해서 네 식구는 먹고
살아갈 수 있었다. 그러나 해순이는 안타까웠다. 물옷
만 입고 나가면 성구 벌이에 못지않을 해순이었다. 어
느 날 밤 해순이는,

"물때가 한창인데……."

"신풀이⁵⁾가 하고 싶나?"

"낼 전복을 좀 딸래……."

"전복은 갈바위 끝으로 가야지?"

"그긴 큰 게 많지……."

"그만둬!"

"가요……."

"못 간다니……."

"집에서 별 할 일도 없는데……."

"놀지……."

"싫에, 낼은 가고 말 게니……."

이래서 해순이가 토라지면 성구는 그만 그 억센 손으
로 해순이를 잡아당겨 토실한 허리가 으스러지도록 껴
안곤 했다.

face to the other's gaze. There had been another time once, even before Haesun had gone away as Sangsu's bride, when her mother-in-law had occasion to say, "Be sure to lock your door before you go to sleep." The memory of that night was much too vivid to Haesun. And her mother-in-law understood well. The caution, 'Be sure to lock your door before you go to sleep,' opened up the past for Haesun.

Haesun was the daughter of a diving woman. After her mother had become pregnant by an itinerant fisherman, she had not been able to leave this village. And then Haesun was born. Haesun grew up following her mother about, seared by the sea breeze in the shadows of the rocks and out on the beaches, or soaking up the smell of salt as she fondled sea shells. From the age of ten she began to learn the art of diving. Haesun married Sŏnggu when she was eighteen. As soon as she had seen her daughter married, Haesun's mother had returned to her home on Jeju Island.

"Because of you I haven't been home for twenty years. But now I can return with an easy heart. Now that you have a husband to serve, you must put all

고등어 철이 왔다. 칠성네 배로 이 마을 고기잡이 여덟 사람이 한 패로 해서 떠나기로 됐다. 이런 때[遠洋出漁]는 되도록이면 같은 고장 사람들끼리 패를 짠다. 같은 날 같이 갔다가 같은 날 같이 돌아온다. 그렇기 때문에 고기잡이 마을에는 같은 달에 난 아이들이 많다. 이 H 마을만 하더라도 같은 달에 난 아이가 다섯이나 된다.

좋은 날씨였다. 뱃전에는 아낙네들이 제가끔 남편들의 어구며 그동안의 신변 연모들을 챙기느라고 부산하다. 사내들은 사내들대로 응당 간밤에 한 말이겠건만, 또 한 번 되풀이를 하곤 한다.

돛이 올랐다. 썰물에 갈바람을 받아 배는 미끄러지기 시작한다. 사내들은 노를 걷고 자리를 잡는다. 뭍을 향해 담배를 붙이려던 만이 아버지는 깜박 잊었다는 듯이 배꼬리로 뛰어오면서 입에 동그라미를 하고 제 아이 이름을 고함쳐 부른다. 아이 대신 그의 아내가 치맛자락을 걷어쥐고 물기슭으로 뛰어들며 귀를 돌린다.

"꼭 그렇게 하라니!"

"멀요?"

"엊밤에 말한 것 말야!"

thoughts of me out of your mind," her mother had said as she set out across the waters on a fishing boat.

Sŏnggu cherished Haesun in marriage as much as he had desired her in courtship. Sŏnggu did not want Haesun to do any outside work. Though their life was not all that prosperous with only Sŏnggu working, the family of four, including his widowed mother and younger brother, managed to survive. All the same, Haesun was dissatisfied. If only she could put on her diving clothes and go out to work, she could earn as much as Sŏnggu. One evening Haesun spoke to him.

"You know, it's the height of the diving season now..."

"You can't get that out of your head, can you?"

"I'm going to catch some abalone tomorrow."

"For abalone don't you have to go out to the end of Sword Rock?"

"Yes, there are lots of big ones there."

"Don't do it."

"I'm going to."

"You won't, I said."

"There's nothing for me to do around the house."

"Then just rest."

"알았소!"

오직 성구만은 돛줄을 잡고 서서 마을 한 모퉁이에 눈을 박고 있다. 거기 돌각담에는 해순이가 손을 뒤로 붙이고 섰다. 갓 온 시집이라 버젓이 뱃전에 나오지 못하는 해순이었다. 성구는 이번 한철 잘하면 기어코 의롱(衣籠)[6]을 한 벌 마련할 작정이었다.

배는 떠났다. 가는 사람이나 보내는 사람이나 그들의 얼굴에는 희망과 기대가 깃들어 있을망정 조그마한 불안의 그림자도 없었다.

바다를 사랑하고, 바다를 믿고, 바다에 기대어 살아온 그들에게는, 기상대나 측후소가 필요치 않았다. 그들의 체험에서 얻은 지식과 신념은 어떠한 이변에도 굽히지 않았다. 날[出漁日]을 받아놓고 선주는 목욕재계하고 풍신과 용신에 제를 올렸다. 풍어(豊漁)도 빌었다. 좋은 날씨에 물때 좋것다, 갈바람이라 무슨 거리낌이 있었으랴!

하늘과 바다가 맞닿는 곳, 솜구름이 양떼처럼 피어오르는 희미한 수평선을 향해 배는 벌써 까마득하다.

대부분의 사내들이 고기잡이로 떠난 갯마을에는 늙은이들이 어린 손자나 데리고 뱃그늘이나 바위 옆에 앉

"No, I don't want to. I'm going tomorrow, and that's that."

When Haesun would get cross like this, Sŏnggu would draw her to him with his strong hands and hug her soft waist tight enough to crush her.

Mackerel season arrived. Eight fishermen of the village formed a group to go out on a fishing boat owned by Ch'ilsŏng's family. Most deep-sea fishing was done by such groups from a single village. They would leave together and return together and so there would be many children born in the same month in these fishing villages. In this one little village alone there had been as many as five children born in the same month.

The weather was fine. Around the gunwales of the boat the women busily packed their husbands' fishing gear and personal belongings. And the men, for their part, were repeating all the things they had told their wives several times the night before.

The sails were raised. Catching the west wind on the ebb-tide, the boat began to move away. The men stowed the sculling oar and took their places. Mani's father, about to light his pipe while gazing toward the mainland, suddenly dashed to the stern

아 무연히 바다를 바라보고, 아낙네들이 썰물에 조개나 캘 뿐 한가하다.

사흘째 되던 날, 윤 노인은 아무래도 수상해서 박 노인을 찾아갔다. 박 노인도 막 물가로 나오는 참이었다. 두 노인은 바위 옆 모래톱에 도사리고 앉았다. 윤 노인이 먼첨 입을 뗐다.

"저 구름발 좀 보라니?"

"음!"

구름발은 동남간으로 해서 검은 불꽃처럼 서북을 향해 뻗어 오르고 있었다.

윤 노인이 또,

"하하아, 저 물빛 봐!"

박 노인은 보라기 전에 벌써 짐작이 갔다. 아무래도 변의 징조였다.

파도 아닌 크고 느린 너울이 왔다. 그럴 때마다 매운 갯냄새가 풍겼다. 틀림없었다.

이번에는 박 노인이 뻔히 알면서도,

"대마도 쪽으로 갔지?"

"고기 떼를 찾아갔는데 울릉도 쪽이면 못 갈라고……."

as if he had forgotten something. Cupping his hands around his mouth, he shouted, "Mani!" But instead of the boy it was his wife who responded. She gathered up her skirt and hurried to the water's edge, cocking an ear towards him.

"Be sure to do as I said!"

"What?"

"What I told you last night!"

"I understand."

Sŏnggu, standing with his hands on the halyard, had his eyes riveted on a spot in the village. There, by the stone wall, Haesun was standing with her hands clasped behind her back. Haesun, the new bride who could not boldly join her husband with the other wives down by the boat. Sŏnggu planned to buy her a new wardrobe chest if this fishing season went well.

The boat was gone. Whether they were the departing fishermen or the ones sending them off, hope and expectation filled their faces without the least shadow of anxiety.

These people who loved the sea, trusted the sea, and depended upon the sea for their livelihood, felt no need of weather forecasts or meteorology. The knowledge and faith they had gained from long ex-

두 노인은 더 말이 없었다. 그새 구름은 해를 덮었다. 바람도 딱 그쳤다. 너울이 점점 커왔다. 큰 너울이 올 적마다 물컥 갯냄새가 코를 찔렀다. 두 노인은 말없이 일어나 헤어졌다. 그들의 경험에는 틀림이 없었다. 올 것은 기어코 오고야 말았다. 무서운 밤이었다. 깜깜한 칠야, 비를 몰아치는 바람과 바다의 아우성—보이는 것은 하늘로 부풀어 오른 파도뿐이었다. 그것은 마치 바다의 참고 참았던 분노가 한꺼번에 터져 흰 이빨로 물을 마구 물어뜯는 거와도 같았다. 파도는 이미 모래톱을 넘어 돌각담을 삼키고 몇몇 집을 휩쓸었다. 마을 사람들은 뒤 언덕배기 당집으로 모여들었다. 이러는 동안에 날이 샜다. 날이 새자부터 바람이 멎어가고 파도도 낮아갔다. 샌 날에 보는 마을은 그야말로 난장판이었다.

이날 밤 한 사람의 희생이 있었다. 윤 노인이었다. 그의 며느리 말에 의하면 돌각담이 무너지고 파도가 축담 밑까지 들이밀자 윤 노인은 며느리와 손자를 앞세우고 담 밖까지 나오다가 무슨 일로선지 며느리에게 먼첨 가라고 하고 윤 노인은 다시 들어갔다고 한다. 그리고는 아무도 모른다.

바다는 언제 그런 일이 있었던가 하듯 잔물결이 안으

perience was unshaken by any adversity. Once the sailing date had been set, the owner of the boat would bathe and purify himself and then offer services to the gods of the wind and water. He would also pray for a big catch. With the weather so fine, the tide would be good and high; and with the westerlies behind them, what possible concerns could they have?

Heading for the faint horizon, where the sky and sea met and cotton clouds rose like a flock of sheep, the boat was already a distant dot.

In this seaside village where most of the young men had gone fishing, the old men took their grand-children to sit with them in the shadows of the boats or among the rocks and there gaze longingly out to sea. And the women just quietly dug clams when the tide was out.

On the third day after the boats had left, Old Man Yun, feeling strangely anxious, sought out Old Man Pak. Old Man Pak, too, was just then coming out to the water's edge. The two old men sat down on the beach by a large rock. Old Man Yun spoke first.

"Take a look at that long cloud there."

"Hmm."

The long cloud, stretching from the southeast to-

로 굽은 모래톱을 찰싹대고, 볕은 한결 뜨거웠고, 하늘
은 남빛으로 더욱 짙었다.

그러나 고등어 배는 돌아오지 않았다. 마을은 더 큰
어두운 수심에 잠겼다. 이틀 뒤에 후리막 주인이 신문
을 한 장 가지고 와서, 출어한 많은 어선들이 행방불명
이 됐다는 기사를 읽어주었다. 마을은 다시 수라장이
됐다. 집집마다 울음소리가 그치지 않았다. 이틀이 지
났다. 울음에도 지쳤다. 울어서 해결될 문제가 아니었
다.

—설마 죽었을라고.

이런 희망을 가지고 아낙네들은 다시 바다로 나갔다.
살아야 했다. 바다에서 죽고 바다로 해서 산다. 해순이
는 성구가 돌아올 것을 누구보다도 믿었다. 그동안 세
식구가 먹고 살아야 했다. 해순이도 물옷을 입고 바다
로 나갔다.

해조를 따고 조개를 캐다가도 문득 이마에 손을 하고
수평선을 바라보곤 아련한 돛배만 지나가도 괜히 가슴
을 두근거리는 아낙네들이었다. 멸치 철이건만 후리도
없었다. 후리막은 집뚜껑을 송두리째 날려버린 그대로
손볼 엄두를 내지 않았다. 후리도 없는 갯마을 여름밤

ward the northwest like a tongue of dark flame, was rising in the sky. Old Man Yun spoke again.

"Ah! Look at the color of that water!"

Even before he was asked to look, Old Man Pak already had his suspicions. However one looked at it, this was a sign of trouble. A large, slow swell— not quite a wave—approached them. And with each swell came the sharp odor of salt. There was no mistaking it.

"They went toward Tsushima, didn't they?" asked Old Man Pak, knowing the answer all along.

"Well, since they were after schooling fish, there's no reason they won't be heading for Ullŭng Island."

The two old men had nothing further to say. In the meantime, the cloud covered the sun. The wind died down. The swells slowly grew larger. Each time a large swell rolled in, the heavy smell of salt stung their nostrils. The two old men silently rose and silently parted. There was no doubting their experience. What was to come most surely came. It was a fearful night. A pitch-black night. The roar of the sea and the rain-driving wind: all that could be seen was waves swelling towards the heavens. It was as if the sea had suddenly unleashed an anger it had held back for ages and was now tearing furi-

을, 아낙네들은 일쑤 불가에 모였다. 장에 갔다 온 아낙
네의 장시세를 비롯해서 보고 들은 이야기―이것이 아
낙네들의 새로운 소식이요 즐거움이었다. 싸늘한 모래
에 발을 묻고 밤새는 줄 몰랐다. 숙이 엄마가 해순이 허
벅지를 베고 벌렁 누우면서,

"에따, 그 베개 편하다……."

그러자 누가,

"그 베개 임자는 어데 갔는고?"

아낙네들의 입에서는 모두 가느다란 한숨이 진다. 숙
이 엄마는 해순이 얼굴을 말끄러미 쳐다보면서,

에에야 데야 에에야 데야

썰물이 돛 달고

갈바람 맞아 갔소.

하자 아낙네들은 모두,

에에야 데야

샛바람 치거던

밀물에 돌아오소

ously at the land with leaping white teeth. The waves had already crossed the beach, devoured the stone wall, and swept away several cottages. The villagers had taken shelter in a shrine high on the hill behind their settlement. By now day had dawned; and with the dawn the wind quieted down and the waves receded. The village revealed by the early light of day was a scene of devastation.

During the night the storm had claimed a victim. It was Old Man Yun. According to his daughter-in-law, Old Man Yun had fetched her and his grandson out beyond their garden wall before the breakwater had collapsed and let the waves push in as far as the embankment. But then, for some unknown reason, he sent them on ahead and went back inside their cottage. They knew of nothing after that.

The sea lapped the deeply curved beach with gentle ripples, forgetful of what had happened. The sunshine was warmer than ever and the sky was an unusually deep indigo.

But the mackerel fishing boat had not returned. The whole village was sunk in dark anxiety. Two days later, the owner of the watch-tower came around with a newspaper from which she read that

에에야 데야.

아낙네들은 그만 목이 메어버린다. 이때,

"떼과부 년들이 모아서 머 시시닥거리노?"

보나마나 칠성네다. 만이 엄마가,

"과부 아닌 게 저러면 밉지나 않제?"

칠성네도 다리를 뻗고 펄썩 앉으면서,

"과부도 과부 나름이지 내사 벌써 사십이 넘었지만,
이년들 괜히 서방 생각이 나서 자도 않고……."

"말도 마소. 이십 전 과부는 살아도, 사십……."

"시끄럽다, 이년들아, 사내 녀석들 한 두름 몰아다 갈
라줄 테니……."

"성님이나 실컷 하소……."

모두 딱따그르 웃는다.

이래저래 여름이 가고 잡어가 많이 잡히는 가을도 헛
되이 보냈다.

모자기, 톳나물, 가스레나물, 파래, 김 해서 한 무렵 가
면 미역 철이다.

미역 철이 되면 해순이는 금보다 귀한 몸이다. 미역은
아무래도 길반쯤 물속이 좋다. 잠수는 해순이밖에 없

many deep-sea fishing boats were unaccounted for. The village was distraught. An unceasing sound of wailing filled each house. After two days they had cried themselves into silence. Nothing was to be solved by their tears.

Surely, they couldn't have died. With one such thread of hope, the women approached the sea again. They had to live. If one could die by the sea, one could also live by the sea. More than anyone else, Haesun had faith that her Sŏnggu would return. In the meantime, there were mouths to be fed. Haesun put on her diving clothes and returned to the sea.

The wives gathered seaweed and dug clams, only to stop suddenly and, shading their eyes with their hands, search the horizon. The faint sign of a passing sail would set their hearts leaping vainly. The anchovy season came again but there was no netting. The roof of the watch-tower had been completely blown away and no thought had been given to its repair. With no netting to do, the women of the seaside village would gather of a summer's night on the sand to listen to a woman who had been to market tell of what she had seen and heard there. This was their source of news and entertain-

다. 해순이가 미역을 베 올리면 뭍에서는 아낙네들이 둘러앉아 오라기[7]를 지어 돌밭에 말린다. 미역도 이삼 월까지면 거의 진다.

어느 날 밤, 해순이는 종일 미역바리[8]를 하고 나무등 치같이 쓰러져 잠이 들었다. 얼마쯤이나 됐을까? 분명 코 짐작이 있는 어떤 압박감에 언뜻 눈을 떴다. 이미 당 한 일이었다. 악! 소리를 지른다는 것이 숨결만 가빠지 고 혀가 말을 듣지 않았다. 대신 사내의 옷자락을 휘감 아 잡았다. 세상없어도 놓지 않을 작정 하고—그러나 해순이의 몸뚱어리는 아리숭한 성구의 기억 속으로 자 꾸만 놓여가고 있었다. 그렇게도 휘감아 잡았던 옷자락 이 모르는 새 놓아졌다.

—아니 내가 이게……

해순이는 제 자신에 새삼스레 놀랐다. 마치 꿈속에서 깨듯 바싹 정신이 들자 그만 사내의 상고머리를 가슴패 기 위에 움켜쥐었다. 사내는 발로 더듬어 문을 찼다.

"그 방에 누꼬?"

시어머니의 잠기 가신 또렷한 소리다. 해순이는 가슴 이 덜컥했다. 그러나 입술에 침을 발라 목을 가다듬었 다.

ment. With their feet buried in the cool sand, they would spend the evening, unaware of the passing time.

Sugi's mother pillowed her head in Haesun's lap and, making herself comfortable, stretched out.

"My, that makes a comfortable pillow!"

"I wonder where that pillow's owner has gone?" asked another woman.

As one, the women let long sighs escape. Sugi's mother stared hard into Haesun's eyes and sang.

E-e-ya, te-ya, e-e-ya, te-ya!
Hoisting sail above the ebbing tide,
They were carried by the westerlies.

The other women joined her.

E-e-ya, te-ya!
When they catch the easterlies,
They'll return on a rising tide.
E-e-ya, te-ya!

The hoarse voices trailed off.

"What is this senseless noise you make? You bunch of widows!"

Without looking they knew it was Ch'ilsŏng's wife.

"If you weren't a widow yourself, that would be a hateful thing to say!" said Mani's mother.

"There are widows and there are widows. I'm al-

"뒷간에 갑니더!"

그러고는 사내의 상고머리를 슬그머니 놓아주고 자
국 소리를 터덕댔다. 이날 밤 해순이는 가슴이 두근거
려 더는 잠을 못 잤다.

다음 날도 미역바리를 나갔다. 숨 가쁜 물속에서도 해
순이 머리 한구석에는 어젯밤 기억이 떠나지 않았다.
돌아오는 길에 성기[9]를 건져다 시어머니에게 국을 끓
여 드렸다. 시어머니는 성깃국을 달갑게 먹으면서,

"얘야, 잘 때는 문을 꼭 닫아걸고 자거라!"

해순이는 고개를 못 들었다. 대답 대신 시어머니 국
대접에 새로 떠온 따신 국만 떠 보탰다.

해순이는 방바위—바위가 둘러싸서 방같이 됐기 때
문에—옆에서 한천(寒天)[10]을 펴고 있었다. 이때 등 뒤
에서,

"해순아!"

해순이는 깜짝 놀라면서 반사적으로 몸을 움츠렸다.
후리막에서 일을 보고 있는 상수다. 해순이는 아랑곳도
않았다. 상수는 슬금슬금 해순이 곁에 다가앉으면서,

"해순이, 내캉 살자!"

ready over forty, you know. But you little ninnies, wasting your time thinking of your men instead of sleeping!" said Ch'ilsŏng's wife, plopping down on the sand with her legs stretched out.

"Hold your tongue! They say a widow under twenty can sleep but a widow over forty..."

"Oh, shut up, you bitches! I'll get you a bunch of men and divide them up among you!"

"Oh, sister, you just have your fill by yourself!"

They all laughed loudly.

The summer passed. They spent the autumn fruitlessly, without the bonuses of fish that netting would have brought them. By the time they had harvested the gulfweed, bladderleaf, kelp, sea lettuce, and laver, it was the season for brown *miyŏk* seaweed.

In *miyŏk* season Haesun was more valuable than gold. The best *miyŏk* came from depths of more than one and a half fathoms. No one in the village but Haesun could dive to such depths. After she had cut the *miyŏk* and brought it to the surface, the other women, sitting in a circle on land, would strip it and lay it out to dry on the rocks. The *miyŏk* season generally ran through February or March.

One night, after a long, hard day of diving for *miyŏk*, Haesun had collapsed into a deep sleep.

상수의 이글거리는 눈이, 물옷만 입은 해순이에게는 온몸에 부시다. 해순이는 암말도 없이 돌아앉았다.

"성구도 없는데 멋 한다고 고생을 하겠노?"

"……."

"내하고 우리 고향에 가 살자! 우리 집엔 논도 있고 밭도 있다!"

사실 그의 고향에는 별 걱정 없이 사는 부모가 있었고, 국민학교를 나온 상수는 농사 돌보고 남부럽지 않게 살았다. 두 해 전에 상처를 하자부터 바람을 잡아 떠돌아다니다가 그의 이모 집인 이 후리막에 와서 뒹굴고 있다.

"은야 해순아!"

상수의 손이 해순이 어깨에 놓였다. 해순이는 탁 뿌리치고 일어났다. 그러나 상수는 어느새 해순이의 팔을 꽉 잡고 놓지 않는다. 실랑이를 하는데 돌아가는 고깃배가 이켠으로 가까워 왔다. 해순이는 바위 그늘에 허리를 꼬부렸다. 그새 상수는 해순이를 끌고 방바위 안으로 숨었다.

"해순이, 우리 날 받아 잔치하자."

"싫에 싫에, 난 싫에!"

How much later might it have been? She suddenly opened her eyes at the sensation of a clearly discernible and rather familiar pressure. It was something she had known before. Instead of a scream she could manage only a gasp—her tongue would not obey. So she grabbed at the man's jacket, winding the cloth around her fists. She tried with all her strength to fend him off, never letting go. But, under the spell of the memory of Sǒnggu, she felt her body relenting little by little. Before she knew it, she had released the jacket.

"Ah, no! What am I..."

She startled even herself with her easy surrender. Gathering her wits as if she had just awoken from a dream, she seized the man by the hair and plunged his head into her breasts. His foot struck the door as he groped in the darkness.

"Who's there?"

There was no trace of sleep in her mother-in-law's sharp voice. Haesun's heart leapt. But she wet her lips and cleared her throat.

"I'm just going to the toilet."

Then she cautiously released the man's hair. She let her mother-in-law hear her noisy footfalls. She could sleep no more that night for the thumping of

"정말?"

"놔요 좀, 해가 지는데……."

"그럼 내 말 한 번만 들어……."

"머 말?"

상수는 해순이 허리에 팔을 돌렸다.

해순이는 몸을 비꼬아 손가락을 비틀었다.

"내 말 안 들으면 소문낼 끼다!"

"머 소문?"

"니하고 내하고 그렇고 그렇다고……."

"……?"

"내 머리 나꾸던 날 밤에……."

해순이는 비로소 알았다. 아무도 모르는 오직 마음속 깊이 간직해 둔 비밀을 옆에서 엿보기나 한 것처럼 해순이는 그만 발끈해지자 허리에 꽂은 조개칼을 뽑아 들었다. 서슬에 상수는 주춤 물러났다. 해순이는 칼을 눈 위에 올려 쥐고,

"내한테 손 대면 찌른다!"

"손 안 델게 내 말 한 번만……."

"소문 낼 텐 안 낼 텐?"

"안 낼게 내 말……."

her heart.

She went out again the next day to dive for *miyŏk*. Even while she was breathless under water, the memory of the night before never once left its corner of Haesun's mind. On the way home that evening she caught some sea urchins, which she boiled up in a soup to give to her mother-in-law. While drinking the soup with pleasure, the mother-in-law spoke.

"Child! Be sure to lock your door when you go to sleep!"

Haesun could not lift her head. Instead of an answer, she ladled more hot soup into her mother-in-law's bowl.

Haesun was next to Chamber Rock—so-called because a circle of rocks seemed to form an enclosure—spreading out sea lettuce. Somebody called from behind her.

"Hey, Haesun!"

Startled, Haesun tensed up. It was Sangsu, who worked at the watch-tower. Haesun would have nothing to do with him. Sangsu sidled up beside her and sat down.

"Haesun, let's you and I live together!" Sangsu's

"나 보고 알은 척 할 텐 안 할 텐?"

"그래 내 말 한 번만 들어주면……."

상수는 칼을 휘두르는 해순이가 겁은커녕 되레 귀여워만 보였다. 해순이는 도사리고 칼을 겨누면서도 그날 밤 기억을 떨어버릴 수가 없었다. 칼 쥔 손이 어느새 턱 밑까지 내렸다. 해순이는 눈시울이 자꾸만 부드러워 갔다.

"해순이!"

하고 상수가 한 걸음 다가오자 해순이는 언뜻 칼을 고쳐 들고 한 걸음 물러난다. 상수가 또 한 걸음 다가오자 해순이는 그만 아무렇게나 칼을 내저으면서,

"더 오지 마래, 더 오면 참말 찌른다!"

"참말 찔리고 싶다. 찌르면 나도 해순이를 안고 같이 죽을 테야!"

하고 상수는 목울대 밑을 가리키면서,

"꼭 요기를 찔러라, 요기를 찔러야 칵 죽는다니……."

해순이는 몸서리를 한번 쳤다. 상수가 또 한 걸음 다가왔다. 그러자 해순이는 바위에 등을 붙이고 울음인지 웃음인지 알 수 없는 소리로,

"안 찌르께 오지 마래!"

blazing eyes sent shivers all through Haesun's body, clad only in her scanty diving suit. Wordlessly, she turned away from him.

"Sŏnggu is gone. Why are you punishing yourself so?"

She did not answer.

"Come with me and live together in my home town. We've got fields and paddies enough."

In fact, both his parents were still living comfortably back home. Sangsu himself had graduated from elementary school and lived well as a farmer with no reason to envy others. When his wife had died two years before, he had left and traveled about until he ended up with his aunt, who owned the watch-tower, and there he had idled since.

"How about it, Haesun?"

Sangsu's hand touched Haesun's shoulder. Haesun shook herself free and stood up. But Sangsu swiftly grabbed Haesun by the arm, holding her tightly. While they were thus occupied, a returning fishing boat passed nearby. Haesun ducked into the shadow of the rocks. In the same moment, Sangsu took hold of Haesun and hid her with him inside Chamber Rock.

"Haesun, let's pick a lucky day and have a cele-

"찔리고 싶어 왼몸이 근질근질하다, 칵 질러라, 그래
서 같이 죽자!"

하는 상수 눈에는 불이 일 듯하면서도 입가에는 어쩌면
미소가 돌 것도 같다. 상수의 눈을 쏘아보던 해순이는
그만 칼을 내던지고,

"참 못됐다!"

상수는 칼을 주워 칼날을 더듬어 보면서,

"내 이 칼 좀 갈아다 줄까. 이 칼로야 어디……."

"어쩌면 저렇게도 못됐을꼬?"

"전복 따듯 목을 싹 도리게시리……."

"흉측해라, 꼭 섬 도둑놈 같다!"

"그랬으면 얼마나 속 시원할꼬?"

"난 갈 테야……."

"날 죽이고 가거라!"

"아이 참, 그럼 어짜라커노?"

"내 말 한 번만……."

"그럼 빨리 말해 보라니……."

상수는 해순이 목에 팔을 감았다. 해순이는 팔꿈으로
뿌리치고 돌아앉아 어깨로부터 물옷을 벗기 시작했다.
이날 해순이는 몇 번이고 상수에게 소문내지 않겠다는

bration."

"No, I don't want to! You're hateful!"

"You really mean that?"

"Let me go! The sun is going down."

"All right, then. Just listen to one thing."

"What's that?"

Sangsu put his arm around Haesun's waist. Haesun twisted her body and bent back his fingers.

"If you don't go along with me, I'll spread the
word."

"What word?"

"About what you and I did together."

"What?"

"That night you grabbed my head..."

Finally, it dawned on her. As if someone had just
ferreted out a dark secret she had long harbored
deep in her heart, Haesun flew into a rage and drew
a clam-opening knife from her belt. At the sudden
turn of her temper, Sangsu withdrew hesitantly.
Haesun brandished the knife before his eyes.

"If you touch me, I'll stab you!"

"I'm not going to touch you. Just listen a moment."

"Are you going to spread rumors or not spread
rumors?"

"I'm not. Now, just—"

다짐을 받았다. 그러나 이틀이 못 가서 아낙네들 새 해순이와 상수가 그렇고 그렇다는 소문이 돌기 시작했다.

고등어 철이 와도 칠성네 배는 소식조차 없었다. 밤이면 아낙네들만이 불가에 모여들었다. 칠성네가 그의 시아버지(박 노인―박 노인은 그 뒤 이렇다 할 병도 없이 시룽시룽 앓아누워 지금껏 자리를 뜨지 못한다)가 시키는 말이라면서 작년 그날을 맞아 일제히 제사를 지내라는 것이었다. 모두 그렇게 하기로 했다. 이 H 마을에 여덟 집 제사가 한꺼번에 드는 셈이다. 제사를 이틀 앞두고 해순이 시어머니는 해순이에게,

"얘야, 성구 제사나 마치거던 개가하두룩 해라!"

"……."

"새파란 청상이 어찌 혼자 늙겠노!"

해순이는 그저 멍했다.

"가면 편할 자리가 있다. 그새 여러 번 말이 있었으나, 성구 첫 제사나 치르고 보자고 해왔다. 너도 대강 짐작이 갈 게다!"

해순이는 낯이 자꾸 달아올랐다. 상수가 틀림없었다. 해순이는 고개가 자꾸만 무거워 갔다.

"과부가 과부 사정을 안다고, 나도 일찍이 홀로 된 몸

"Are you going to act familiar with me in public or not?"

"I know, I know. But if you would just listen to me for a moment..."

The knife-wielding Haesun, far from frightening Sangsu, simply looked the more lovely to him. Haesun began to calm down. Even while threatening him with the knife, she could not shake off the memory of that night. The hand holding the knife sunk below her chin before she was aware of it. The cast of her eyes softened more and more.

"Haesun!"

But as soon as Sangsu took a step closer to Haesun, she quickly raised her knife again and took a step backwards. Sangsu took another step closer but Haesun just waved her knife wildly.

"Don't come any closer! It you do, 1 swear I'll stab you!"

"And I swear I'd like to get stabbed! If you stab me then I'll hold you in my arms and we'll die together!" said Sangsu, pointing to a spot below his adam's apple. "Stab me here and I'll die right off..."

Haesun gave a shudder. Sangsu took another step closer. Then, Haesun leaned against the rock and spoke in a voice halfway between a sob and a laugh.

이라 그 사정 다 안다. 죽은 자식보다 너가 더 애처롭다. 저것(시동생)도 인젠 배를 타고 하니 설마 두 식구야……."

다음 날은 벌써 상수가 해순이를 맞아 간다는 소문이 온 마을에 쫙 퍼졌다. 그러면서도 아낙네들은 해순이마저 떠난다는 것이 진정 섭섭했고 맥이 풀렸다. 눈물을 글썽대는 아낙네도 있었다. 해순이는 이 마을—더구나 아낙네들의 귀염둥이다. 생김새도 밉지 않거니와 마음에 그늘이 없다. 남을 의심할 줄도 모르고 거짓도 없다. 그보다도 우선 미역 철이 오면…… 아낙네들은 절로 한숨이 잦았다. 그러나 해순이는 그저 남녀가 한 번 관계를 맺으면 으레 그렇게 되나 보다, 그래서 그렇게 됐고 또 그렇게 해야 되나 보다—이러는 동안에 후리막 안주인과 상수를 따라 해순이는 가야 했다.

해순이마저 떠난 갯마을은 더욱 쓸쓸했다. 한 길 물속에 미역발을 두고도 철을 놓쳐버렸다. 보릿고개가 장히도 고됐다. 해조로 끼니를 이어가는 집도 한두 집이 아니었다.

또 고등어 철이 왔다. 두 번째 닿는 제사를 사흘 앞두

"I'm not going to stab you. But don't come any closer!"

"I want to get stabbed! My whole body itches for it. Stick it right in and let's die together!" said Sangsu. His eyes lit with fire but a tender smile played around his lips.

Haesun, who had been looking daggers into Sangsu's eyes, finally threw down the knife.

"You're really wicked!"

Sangsu picked up the knife and felt the edge of its blade.

"Shall I sharpen this knife a bit for you? What use is this dull thing?"

"How can you be so wicked?"

"So, you would slit my throat like you cut open an abalone?"

"You are horrible! Just like one of those pirates who prey on the islands!"

"What a delight—if only that were so!"

"I'm going."

"Kill me before you go!"

"Oh, lord! What do you want of me?"

"Just hear me out one time."

"All right. But make it quick!"

Sangsu wrapped his arms around Haesun's neck.

고 아낙네들은 불가에 모였다.

"요번 제사에는 고동 생복도 없겠다!"

"이밥은 못 차려도 바다를 베고서……."

"바닷귀신이 고동 생복 없이는 응감[11]도 않을걸!"

이렇게들 주거니 받거니 하는데 뒤에서 누가,

"왁!"

해순이었다.

"이거 새댁이 앙이가!"

"새댁이 우짠 일고?"

"제사라고 왔나?"

"너거 새서방은?"

그중에서도 숙이 엄마는 해순이를 친정 온 딸이나처
럼 두 손으로 얼굴을 싸고 들여다보면서,

"좀 예빘(여위었)구나?"

그러자 칠성네가,

"여기 좀 앉거라, 보자!"

해순이는 아낙네들에 둘러싸여 비로소,

"성님들 잘 기셨소?"

했다.

"너거 시어머니 봤나?"

Haesun pushed him away with her elbow, sat down with her back to him and began to slip her diving suit off her shoulders. Several times that day Haesun extracted Sangsu's assurances that he wouldn't spread any rumors. But within two days a rumor was passing among the women that Haesun and Sangsu were up to something.

Though the mackerel season came again there was no word of Ch'ilsŏng's boat. In the evenings the women gathered on the sands. Ch'ilsŏng's wife passed on a request from her father-in-law (Old Man Pak, who had been confined to his bed with an unknown disease ever since the storm) that they hold a memorial service on the anniversary of the storm. All agreed to do so and, as a result, eight households in the village held services at the same time. Two days before the services, Haesun's mother-in-law spoke to her.

"Child, after you have held a service for Sŏnggu, why don't you see about marrying again? Why should a healthy young widow like you grow old alone?"

Haesun listened dumbly.

"If you get married, there'll be a comfortable place waiting for you. The subject has come up several times but I wanted to wait until we had passed the

해순이는 고개만 끄덕였다.

그의 시어머니는 해순이를 보자 일부러 실룩이고 눈물을 가두었다. 아들 생각을 해선지? 아니면 제삿날을 잊지 않고 온 며느리가 기특해선지? 해순이는 제 방에 들어가서 우선 잠수 연모부터 찾아보았다. 시렁 위에 그대로 얹혀 있었다. 해순이는 반가웠다. 맘이 놓였다. 그래서 불가로 나왔다.

"난 인자 안 갈 테야, 성님들하고 같이 살 테야!"

그리고는 훌쩍 일어서서 바다를 보고 가슴 가득히 숨을 들이켰다. 오래간만에 맡는, 그렇게도 그립던 갯냄새였다.

아낙네들은 모두 서로 눈만 바라보고 말이 없었다.

상수도 징용으로 끌려가버린 산골에는 견딜 수 없는 해순이었다.

오뉴월 콩밭에 들어서면 깝북 숨이 막혔다. 바랭이풀을 한골 뜯고 나면 손아귀에 맥이 탁 풀렸다. 그럴 때마다 눈앞에 훤히 바다가 틔어 왔다.

물옷을 입고 철벙 뛰어들면…… 해순이는 못 견디게 바다가 아쉽고 그리웠다.

—고등어 철—해순이는 그만 호미를 내던지고 산비

58

first memorial service. You have an idea of whom I have in mind."

Haesun's face flushed. It was, of course, Sangsu. Her head drooped lower and lower.

"Only a widow really understands a widow's plight. I was also left alone early in my life. I know all too well. I feel more pity for you than for my dead son. My younger son will be shipping out one of these days and so, with only two mouths to feed..."

By the next day, word had spread throughout the village that Haesun was going off with Sangsu. But, at the same time, the women were genuinely disappointed and sad to loose their Haesun. Some of the women were even tearful at the news. Haesun was the darling of the village, particularly among the women. Not only was she pleasant to behold, she could not have been more cheerful. She accepted others at their face value and was free of falseness herself. Furthermore, when *miyŏk* season came again—the sighs of the women were redoubled at the thought. But, from Haesun's point of view, once a man and woman had a relationship, that was the way it had to be. Therefore, since what was done was done, there were no two ways about it. So Haesun had to follow Sangsu and his aunt, the

탈로 올라갔다. 그러나 바다는 안 보였다. 해순이는 더욱 기를 쓰고 미칠 듯이 산꼭대기로 기어올랐다. 그래도 바다는 안 보였다.

이런 일이 있은 뒤로 마을에서는 해순이가 매구[12] 혼이 들렸다는 소문이 자자했다.

시가에서 무당을 데려다 굿을 차리는 새, 해순이는 걷은 소매만 내리고 마을을 빠져나와 삼십 리 산길을 단걸음에 달려온 것이다.

"너 진정이냐? 속 시원히 말 좀 해라, 보자."

숙이 엄마의 좀 다급한 물음에도, 해순이는 조용조용,

"수수밭에 가면 수숫대가 모두 미역발 같고, 콩밭에 가면 콩밭이 왼통 바다만 같고……."

"그래?"

"바다가 보고파 자꾸 산으로 올라갔지 머, 그래도 바다가 안 보이데."

"그래 너거 새서방은?"

"징용 간 지가 언제라고……."

"저런……."

"시집에선 날 매구 혼이 들렸대."

"쫏쫏."

owner of the watch-tower.

With Haesun gone, the seaside village felt deso-
late. The patch of *miyŏk* lying under a fathom of
water was left untouched as its season came and
went. The spring food shortage was quite as bad as
the year before and more than a few households
had to make do on a diet of seaweed.

The mackerel season came once again. Three
days before the memorial services on the second
anniversary of the storm, the women gathered
again on the sands.

"There'll be no fresh mackerel or abalone meat
for the altar this time."

"There's no rice to serve, but we do have the sea
at our doorsteps..."

"The spirits of the sea certainly won't be ap-
peased without fresh mackerel and abalone!"

While the women talked among themselves, a
figure suddenly appeared from beyond them. It was
Haesun.

"Isn't this our new bride?"

"What brings you back?"

"You came for the services?"

"Where's the new groom?"

"난 인제 죽어도 안 갈 테야, 성님들하고 여기 같이 살 테야!"

이때 후리막에서 야단스레 꽹과리가 울렸다.

"아, 후리다!"

"후리다!"

"안 가?"

"왜 안 가!"

숙이 엄마가 해순이를 보고,

"맴치마만 두르고 빨리 나오라니……."

해순이는 재빨리 옷을 갈아입고 나왔다. 아낙네들은 해순이를 앞세우고 후리막으로 달려갔다. 맨발에 식은 모래가 해순이는 오장육부에 간지럽도록 시원했다.

달음산 마루에 초아흐레 달이 걸렸다. 달그림자를 따라 멸치 떼가 들었다.

—데에야 데야.

드물게 보는 멸치 떼였다.

1) 후리막. 후릿그물을 치고, 그것을 지키기 위해 지은 막. 후릿그물은 강이나 바다에 넓게 둘러치고 여러 사람이 두 끝을 끌어당겨 물고기를 잡는 큰 그물.
2) 이리꼬. 말린 멸치를 뜻하는 일본어.
3) 사르개. 불이 살아나게 하는 것.
4) 성례. 혼인의 예식을 지냄.

All the women were glad to see her, but Sugi's mother greeted Haesun as she might her own daughter on the first visit home after marrying.

"You've grown a little thin!" she said, cradling Haesun's face in her hands.

"Sit down here and let's have a look at you!" added Ch'ilsŏng's wife.

"Have you been well, sisters?" began Haesun, encircled by the women.

"Have you seen your mother-in-law?"

Haesun merely nodded. When Haesun had sought out her mother-in-law, the woman's lips trembled and tears welled up in her eyes. Could it have been for thoughts of her son? Could she have been overwhelmed by a daughter-in-law who had not forgotten to return for her son's memorial service? The first thing Haesun had done was to look for the diving gear in her room. It was waiting, untouched, on the shelf. Haesun was relieved and happy. Only then had she gone out to the sands.

"I'm not going back. I'm going to live here with my sisters!"

With that, she suddenly rose and, gazing out at the sea, breathed deeply. It had been a long time since she had breathed that salty air for which she

5) 신풀이. 신들린 사람을 위하여 푸닥거리를 하는 일.

6) 의롱(衣籠). 옷농. 옷을 넣어두는 농.

7) 오라기. 실, 헝겊, 종이, 새끼 따위의 길고 가느다란 조각.

8) 미역바리. 미역 따는 일.

9) 성기. 성게.

10) 한천(寒天). 우뭇가사리.

11) 응감. 마음에 응하여 느낌.

12) 매구. 천 년 묵은 여우가 변하여 된다는 전설에서의 짐승.

* 작가 고유의 문체나 당시 쓰이던 용어를 그대로 살려 원문에
최대한 가깝게 표기하고자 하였다. 단, 현재 쓰이지 않는 말이
나 띄어쓰기는 현행 맞춤법에 맞게 표기하였다.

《문예(文藝)》, 1953

had yearned so much. The women exchanged silent glances.

Haesun could not endure life in that mountain village after Sangsu had been dragged away to the army. She felt smothered as she stood in the hot bean fields of May and June. After weeding a furrow she could feel the strength go out of her grip. And, each time, a vision of the sea would rise before her eyes. If she could just put on her diving clothes and leap in! Haesun missed her beloved sea beyond endurance.

When the mackerel season came, Haesun threw down her hoe and climbed the mountain slope. But no sea met her eyes. Driven, Haesun, crawled madly to the top of the mountain. But still there was no ocean to be seen.

After this incident, a rumor that Haesun was possessed made the rounds of the village. When her husband's people brought in a *mudang* from the marketplace and were making ready for an exorcism, Haesun simply rolled down her sleeves, slipped out of the village, and ran the thirty *li* over mountain paths back to the sea without stopping.

"Do you really mean it? Tell us about it to set our minds at ease."

Against the urgency of Sugi's mother's question came Haesun's slow and quiet reply.

"When I went into the millet field, the stalks of millet all looked like *miyŏk*; and when I went into the bean field, it looked only like the sea..."

"Really!"

"I wanted so much to see the ocean. I kept climbing up the mountain, but there was no ocean to be seen."

"But what about your new husband?"

"Taken in the draft—when would I see him again?"

"Good lord!"

"My in-laws kept saying I was possessed."

"Oh, no!"

"I'd sooner die than go back now. I'm going to stay here and live with you!"

At this moment, a gong rang out loudly from the watch-tower.

"Ah! Netting!"

"Netting!"

"Aren't you going?"

"Of course I'm going!"

"Just throw on an outer skirt and come quickly!" said Sugi's mother to Haesun.

Haesun changed her clothes quickly and came

back out. The women, with Haesun in the lead, ran toward the watch-tower. The cool sand touching her bare feet cooled her all over.

A half-moon hung over the ridge of Tarŭm Mountain. A school of anchovies had followed the moon's light to shore.

Te-e-ya, te-ya!

It was a school of anchovies such as they had seldom seen.

Translated by Marshall R. Pihl

해설

Afterword

푸른 해원(海原)을 향한 영원한 노스탤지어

김종욱 (문학평론가)

오영수의 소설 「갯마을」은 바닷가 마을에서 멸치를 잡는 현재의 시간에서 시작하여 주인공 해순이 과거에 겪었던 여러 사건들을 제시하는 방식으로 구성되어 있다. 첫 남편이 고등어잡이를 나가 풍랑으로 돌아오지 못하자 상수의 구혼을 받아들여 재혼한 후 갯마을을 떠났지만, 향수병에 걸려 다시 갯마을로 돌아오는 지난 일들이 순차적으로 그려지고 있는 것이다. 그런데 소설의 끝에 해당하는 멸치떼를 좇는 장면은 첫 방면과 잇닿아 있어서 순환을 이루는 것처럼 보인다.

이러한 구성은 형식적인 완결성을 높일 뿐만 아니라 갯마을 사람들의 삶의 방식을 보여주는 것이기도 하다.

Yearning for the Blue Sea

Kim Jong-uk (literary critic)

Oh Yeongsu's "Seaside Village" opens in the present tense at a seaside village engaged in anchovy fishing, with the protagonist, Hae-sun, recounting several episodes from her past. Her first husband had gone mackerel fishing in his boat, never to come back. She then accepted the suitor Sang-su's proposal, remarried, and left the village, only to return after feeling homesick. These episodes are narrated in sequence, with the first scene of catching anchovies mirrored in the last in a circular form.

This structure of the story not only heightens its formal integrity but also shows the way of life in the village. An episode in the opening scene foreshad-

첫 장면에 해순이 상수를 만났을 때를 연상시키는 사건이 삽입되어 있어서 해순에게 앞으로도 비슷한 일이 반복되리라고 암시하는 것이다. 갯마을에서의 삶을 지배하는 반복성은 이뿐만이 아니다. 세대를 뛰어넘어 해순 모녀의 삶도 매우 닮아 있다. 어머니가 자식 때문에 이 마을에 머물러 살다가 딸이 시집을 가자 고향 바다로 돌아갔던 것처럼 해순 역시 산골에 시집을 갔다가 끝내 고향에 돌아왔던 것이다.

이러한 반복성 때문에 「갯마을」에서 시간은 사람들에게 큰 의미를 지니지 못한다. 시간은 끊임없이 흘러가지만 삶을 변화시키지는 못하기 때문이다. 그것을 갯마을 사람들의 '운명'이라고 부를 수 있을 터인데, 사람들은 자신에게 부여된 운명에 순응하며 삶을 견뎌내는 것만이 허용되어 있을 뿐이다. 이처럼 운명적 시간을 대신하여 갯마을 사람들의 삶에 큰 영향을 미치는 것은 공간이다. '바다 여인'이라는 의미를 담고 있는 이름이 암시하듯이 해순은 마음의 고향으로서의 갯마을을 떠나서는 살아갈 수 없다. 갯마을은 생활의 터전일 뿐만 아니라 삶의 의미 그 자체였던 것이다.

이렇듯 고향을 향한 애착과 동경은 오영수 소설의 중

ows Hae-sun's meeting Sang-su, hinting that a similar occurrence will happen to her in the future. And this is not the only event that recurs in the village. The lives of Hae-sun and her mother also follow a pattern repeated generation after generation. After Hae-sun's marriage, her mother, who had stayed in the village for her daughter's sake, returns to her own hometown, which is also by the sea. Then Hae-sun also gravitates back to her hometown, after her second marriage in a mountain village.

Because of this repetition, time does not hold much meaning for the characters. Instead it ebbs and flows without noticeable effect on their lives. One might call it the characters' "destinies." They have no choice but to accept their preordained fates and endure it. Compared to this fatalistic time, though, space has an important effect on the lives of characters in the seaside village. For instance, Hae-sun, whose name means "sea's woman," cannot live away from the village. The sea is not simply a source of livelihood but the source of life's meaning.

The affinity and longing for one's hometown is a key feature of Oh Yeongsu's fictional world. The

요한 특징이다. 고향은 언제 찾아가도 변하지 않는 모습으로 사람들을 맞이하는 어머니의 품과 같다. 물론 그곳이 삶의 괴로움과 아픔이 없는 완전한 유토피아라는 의미는 아니다. 해순은 첫 번째 남편을 바다에서 잃게 되자 절망과 아픔 속에서 고향을 떠났다. 하지만 바다를 떠난다고 해서 행복했던 것은 아니다. 산골에서의 새로운 생활도 남편의 징용으로 불행한 결말로 이어지고 말았던 것이다. 따라서 그녀가 겪는 고난은 갯마을에서 살았기 때문이 아니라 삶 자체가 고해(苦海)였기 때문이다. 그 대신 고향은 이러한 괴로움과 아픔을 함께 나누고 견뎌낼 수 있는 힘을 준다. 고향은 인간적인 유대가 살아 있어서 각 개인들에게 찾아오는 고통과 절망을 서로 위로하고 함께 이겨낼 수 있도록 만드는, 작지만 소중한 공동체인 것이다.

오영수가 그려낸 이러한 공동체는 전쟁의 상처로 고통받고 있던 당대의 독자들에게 큰 위안을 주었다. 이 작품이 처음 발표된 것은 한국전쟁이 멈춘 직후였던 1953년 12월이었다. 당시 발표된 소설들이 대부분 전쟁 직후의 암울한 현실을 그린 것과 비교해 볼 때, 이 작품이 평화로운 어촌을 배경으로 자연의 질서에 순응하며

hometown is like the outstretched arms of a mother drawing one into her embrace. This does not mean that it is paradise, however, free from suffering and pain. After all, the protagonist left her village in despair and hurt when she lost her husband. But happiness eluded her away from the village. Her new life in the mountains ended without joy when her second husband was drafted into the military. Thus, her suffering had nothing to do with where she lived, because life itself was suffering. However, her hometown actually gives her the strength to carry on and share in the pain and suffering of other people. It is a small but sheltered community, a place of human warmth where people comfort and sustain each other through their hardships and misery.

The kind of village depicted by Oh Yeongsu is a comfort to many readers whose own communities suffered scars from the Korean War. "Seaside Village" was published in December 1953, shortly after the war ended in a truce. Given that most works of fiction published at this time dwelt on the bleak realities in the aftermath of the war, "Seaside Village" stands out because it tells the story of innocent and warmhearted people living with nature in a peace-

따스한 인정을 간직한 사람들을 그리고 있다는 점은 매우 중요하다. 그곳에서는 참혹한 전쟁을 일으켰던 이데올로기 대립도 찾아볼 수 없고, 사람들의 본성을 억압하는 윤리 규범도 발견할 수 없다. 해순의 애정관계에서 잘 드러나듯이, 사람들은 자신의 성정에 따라 자연스럽게 사랑을 하고 기쁨과 슬픔을 나누며 살아가는 것이다. 이처럼 독자들은 「갯마을」을 읽으면서 언제든지 자신을 따듯하게 맞아줄 고향에 대한 상상으로 피난의 아픔을 잠시나마 잊을 수 있었던 것이다.

하지만 고향에 대한 애착과 동경이 작품의 전면에 부각되어 있다는 점은 비판의 대상이 되기도 한다. 「갯마을」에서 풍랑으로 남편을 잃은 갯마을 여인들의 현실이 한(恨)이라는 이름으로 추상화되면서 절박함을 잃어버렸다는 것이다. 또는 전통적인 공동체가 근대화와 함께 점차 소멸되어가는 현실을 무시하고 공동체로의 복귀를 강하게 열망하고 있다는 점에서 낭만적이거나 시대착오적이라는 것이다. 이러한 비판은 오영수에 대한 편협한 인식에서 비롯한 것이다. 오영수는 「갯마을」 이후에 「메아리」(1959), 「은냇골 이야기」(1961) 등을 통해 고향으로의 무조건적인 복귀가 아니라 자신들만의 공

ful seaside community. There is no mention of conflicting ideologies, which could spark a disastrous war, or a code of ethics that runs counter to human nature. As the protagonist Hae-sun's viewpoint shows, people fall in love as they live and share in each other's pleasures and sorrows. The story's readers could forget the pain of war, however briefly, by conjuring a hometown that would warmly welcome them any time.

The longing and nostalgia for one's hometown found in Oh Yeongsu's work have also drawn criticism though. The plight of the women in "Seaside Village" who lost their husbands to the sea is referred to simply as 'han,' Korean for sorrow, and is stripped of its sense of desperation. It has been criticized as romanticized and idealized, as the author depicts a longing for a return to community, ignoring the gradual disappearance of the traditional community with the coming of modernization. But such criticism stems from a superficial understanding of Oh Yeongsu's works. In "Echo" (1959) and "A Story About Eunnae Village" (1961) his characters build their own community instead of simply returning to their hometown. One could even say that rather than longing for a return to the past, Oh's

동체를 만들어가는 과정을 그리고 있다. 실제로 오영수가 꿈꾸었던 자연 혹은 공동체적인 삶은 시간을 거슬러 올라가는 퇴행적인 성격보다는 적자생존의 원리가 지배하는 현실을 넘어서려는 비판적인 성격을 보여준다. 이러한 문명비판적인 태도는 해방 직후 오영수가 활동했던 조선청년문학가협회 경남지부, 특히 유치환의 아나키즘적 성향에서 적지 않은 영향을 받은 것으로 보인다.

vision of nature and communal life is an indictment of the harsh reality governed by the principle of the survival of the fittest, and an attempt to show that people can opt out of this reality. This critical stance toward civilization seems to have been largely influenced by Oh's activities in the Gyeong-nam chapter of the Joseon Young Writers' Association after Korea's independence from Japan, especially by its leader Yu Chi-hwan's anarchism.

비평의 목소리

Critical Acclaim

한국적 리리시즘의 작가로 불리는 오영수의 문학은 무시간성의 세계에 폐쇄되어 있다. 현재시제를 주로 사용하는 서술의 특이함이 이에 대응하는데, 과거시제의 거부란 곧 서사의 거부인 것이다. 서사를 거부함으로써 오영수가 노리는 것은 시류와는 무관하게 변하지 않는 '인간성', 인간과 자연이 조화롭게 어울리는 문명 이전의 원시적 '순진성'을 강조하는 것이다. 그러므로 오영수의 소설에서 복잡한 현실 법칙과 이것을 따라 영위되는 생활을 찾을 수 없다. 그것들과는 무관한, 그 이전의 본래적인 것만이 문제되기 때문이다.

김윤식 · 정호웅, 『한국소설사』, 문학동네, 2000

The works of Oh Yeongsu, a writer known for his lyricism, inhabit a timeless realm. This is confirmed by his partiality toward the present tense. His refusal to use the past tense is a form of protest against traditional narrative. By denying narrative, he aims at highlighting the immutability of humanity in the face of modern trends, as well as the primitive innocence of the past, in which human beings lived in harmony with nature. Therefore, the reader will be disappointed if he or she searches for characters bound by the complex rules of reality in his fiction, because they are represented as irrelevant to the essentials of life.

오영수는 「화산댁이」와 「갯마을」을 통해 자기 작품 세계를 확립한다. 그의 소설은 토속적 공간을 배경으로 하여 그 속에 살고 있는 순박한 인간들의 인정미를 추구하는 경우가 많다. 그렇기 때문에 어떤 작품에서는 반문명적인 자연 예찬이 과장되어 나타나기도 하고, 향촌에 대한 애정이 심정적인 진술을 통해 제시되기도 한다. 한편 오영수는 「박학도」 「후조」 「명암」 등에서 살벌한 현실에 얽매어 자기 존재의 진정한 의미를 잃어버린 채 살아가는 인간의 비애를 그려보임으로써, 특유의 서정성과 현실인식의 두 경향을 유지하고 있는 것처럼 보인다. 그러나 어떤 경우이든지 간에 오영수의 소설은 그 규모에 있어서 단편성을 모면하지 못하고 있으며, 이른바 산문정신의 결여 상태라고 할 수 있는 서정성에의 함몰을 드러내고 있는 경우가 많다.

권영민, 『한국현대문학사』2, 민음사, 2002

오영수가 시종 응시한 지점은, 혹은 그 연민의 시선의 발원 지점은, 총알에 관통당한 머루의 형상이다. 이 응집점에 평화 속의 전쟁, 전쟁 속의 평화의 다양한 프리즘이 분광된다. 「오지에서 온 편지」 등 다수의 소설에서

Kim Yun-shik and Chung Ho-ung,

The History of Korean Fiction (Seoul: Munhak Dongnae, 2000)

Oh Yeongsu carved out a place in the literary
world with the publication of "The Woman from
Hwasan" and "Seaside Village." Set in indigenous lo-
cations, his fiction seeks to reveal his characters'
innocence and humanity. As a result, some of his
works eulogize nature to the point of seeming to
be against civilization. His portrayal of the countryside is unfailingly sympathetic. Meanwhile, he depicts the wretchedness of human beings trapped in
cruel situations without being able to find the meaning of their existence in "Light and Darkness," "Mi-
gratory Birds," and "Park Hak-do." These works
show his consciousness of reality in addition to his
trademark lyricism. Nonetheless, his fiction does
not overcome a lopsidedness in scale, because his
preoccupation with lyricism detracts from the pro-
saic spirit of his narrative.

Kwon Young-min, *The History of Modern Korean Literature*

Vol. 2 (Seoul: Minumsa, 2002)

Oh Yeongsu's sympathetic gaze rests on images
such as wild grapes that become riddled with bul-

보이는 생태학적 상상력도, 다시 말해 자연으로 돌아가고 싶어 한 자연친화적인 상상력도, 실은 총알에 의해 관통당하기 이전의 '머루 익는 마을의 사랑'에 대한 한없는 그리움에 기인한 바 크다. 오영수 소설에는 전쟁과 평화, 사회성과 서정성, 문명성과 자연성 등에 복합적으로 융합되어 있다. 결코 단순한 농촌 작가가 아니었던 것이다.

우찬제, 「'총알'과 '머루'의 상호텍스트성」,

《문학과환경》 8권 1호, 2009

고향/도시; 장소/공간; 경험/체험의 대립쌍은 오영수의 문학을 해명하는 데 유용한 방법이 된다. 그의 문학적 역정은 고향이 부여한 영속적이고 신화적인 장소의 경험을 간직하면서 도시 공간의 낯섦과 비인간화를 견뎌내면서 마침내 참된 장소를 찾아가는 과정을 보이고 있다. 그에게 내부의 장소감은 창작의 원동력이다. 또한 그러한 장소에 대한 경험적 지향으로 그의 소설은 서정화될 뿐만 아니라 공동의 경험을 나누는 이야기성을 담보한다. 이러한 점에서 그는 장소 파괴와 무장소성이 일반화되고 있는 현대에 저항하면서 새로운 가치

lets. This stark point of convergence diffuses into various "prisms," like war in peace and peace in war. His ecological imagination, evident in many of his stories and his love of the environment and a longing to return to nature, stem from an eternal longing for the village, where wild grapes ripen, before a bullet may tear them apart. War and peace, society and lyricism, civilization and nature intertwine in a complex way in his fiction. He is not simply a writer of the countryside.

Woo Chan-je, "Intertextuality of Bullets and Wild Grapes," *Literature and Environment*, 8.1, 2009

The dualities of hometown/city, place/space, and experience/direct experience are an effective way of viewing the literature of Oh Yeongsu. His oeuvre shows how he manages to find a genuine place by overcoming the strangeness of urban space and inhumanity, while retaining the experience of eternal and mythical space in the hometown. For him, a sense of inner space is a motive for creative writing. The longing to inhabit such a place not only lyricizes his fiction but also secures the narrative for communal experience. In this regard, he should be recognized anew as a writer who poses the key is-

의 공동체를 구성하는 21세기적 과제를 던지고 있는 작
가로 재인식되어야 한다.

구모룡, 「난계 오영수의 유기론적 문학사상에 관한 시론」,

《영주어문》 20집, 2010.8

sue of the 21st century: How to create a community of new values by resisting the modern situation that destroys place and gives primacy to placelessness.

Koo Mo-ryong, "Criticism on Oh Yeongsu's Organic Literary Philosophy," *Youngju Language and Literature*, Vol. 20, August, 2010

오영수

　오영수는 1909년 2월 11일 경상남도 울주군 언양면에서 출생하였다. 향리에서 한학(漢學)을 공부하다가 뒤늦게 언양보통학교에 입학하였는데, 이 무렵《동아일보》《조선일보》에 동시를 발표하면서 문학적 재질을 보여주었다. 그 후, 일본에 건너가 오사카에 있는 나니와중학(浪速中學) 속성과에 다녔지만, 어려운 가정 형편 때문에 대학에 진학하지 못한 채 귀국했다. 1935년 다시일본에 건너가 도쿄국민예술원(東京國民藝術院)을 수료하였다. 1940년대 초 만주 등지를 방랑하다가 귀국하여부산 인근에서 교편을 잡았다.

　해방 후에는 부산 지역의 문학 단체에 참여하는 한편《백민》에 시를 발표하기도 하였다. 1949년《신천지》에「남이와 엿장수」를 발표하면서 소설로 전향하였다. 한국전쟁 중에는 유치환 등과 함께 종군작가로 참여한 뒤서울에 올라와 1955년부터《현대문학》편집장으로 10여 년 동안 활동하였다. 이후 30여 년 동안 작가생활을하면서『머루』(1954),『갯마을』(1956),『명암(明暗)』(1958),

Oh Yeongsu

Oh Yeongsu was born in Eonyang, Ulju-gun, Gyeongsangnam-do on February 11, 1909. He began his education at a traditional Confucian school, then entered Eonyang Elementary School. During this period, he showed his literary talents by publishing children's poems in the *Dong-A Ilbo* and the *Chosun Ilbo*. Later, he went to Japan to attend an intensive program at Naniwa Middle School in Osaka, but could not afford to go to college because of financial difficulties, so returned home. He returned to Japan in 1935 to complete a course at the Tokyo National Arts Academy. He wandered around Manchuria in the early 1940s, then returned to Korea, taking up teaching at a school near Busan. After Korea's liberation from Japan, he joined literary groups in Busan and published his poetry in *Baekmin*. He shifted to fiction writing in 1949, publishing "Nami and Taffy Man" in *New World*. During the Korean War, he served as a war correspondent together with Yu Chi-hwan. He moved to Seoul in 1955, and worked as managing editor of *the Modern*

『메아리』(1960), 『수련(睡蓮)』(1965), 『황혼』(1976), 『잃어버린 도원(桃園)』(1978) 등 7권의 단편집을 출간하였다. 1978년부터 예술원 회원으로 활동하다가 1979년 5월 15일 사망했다.

　오영수는 전쟁 직후의 암울한 현실을 묘사하고자 했던 1950년대 젊은 작가들과 달리 향토적 공간을 배경으로 하여 그 속에 살고 있는 순박한 인간들의 인정미를 추구하였다. 그래서 그의 작품에 등장하는 주인공들은 대부분 세상의 질서에 현명하게 대처하지 못하는 가난하고 어리숙한 인물들이다. 타락한 현대의 도시문명에 오염되지 않은 건강한 인간성에 대한 향수를 어린이, 농촌, 자연 등으로 환치시키고 있는 것이다. 반공주의에 기대어 국가의 이익을 우선시하고 과학기술을 통해서만 문명이 발전할 수 있다는 믿음만을 강요하던 시대적 분위기에서, 이처럼 개인의 선한 본성이 살아 숨쉬는 세계를 지향한다는 점에서 오영수는 여전히 문제적인 작가라고 할 수 있다.

Literature for more than ten years. In a span of more than 30 years, he published seven short-story collections: *Wild Grapes* in 1954, *Seaside Village* in 1956, *Light and Darkness* in 1958, *Echo* in 1960, *Water Lily* in 1965, *Dusk* in 1976, and *Lost Peach Garden* in 1978. He was appointed to the Academy of Arts in 1978 and died on May 15, 1979.

Unlike other young writers in the 1950s, who sought to portray the dismal reality in the wake of the Korean War, Oh attempted to impart the humanity of ordinary people against the backdrop of the countryside. As such, most of his protagonists are poor, naive characters who lack the cunning to rise in the world. His nostalgia for simple humanity, uncorrupted by modern urban civilization, is transposed into children, the countryside, and nature. Oh posed a lot of questions as he envisioned a world where the goodness of human beings prevailed—at a time when people were pressured to believe that the nation could enjoy progress only by embracing science and technology, putting national interests ahead of personal well-being, and relying on an anti-communist ideology.

번역 **마샬 필** Translated by Marshall R. Pihl

마샬 필은 1957년 서울에 주둔하고 있던 한국 군사고문단의 공보장교로 배치되었을 때 처음으로 한국을 접했다. 1960년 하버드 대학교를 졸업하고 월간지인 《사상계》의 연구부에 합류하기 위해서 한국에 갔고, 사상계사에서 잡지사의 직원들의 후견 아래 논문과 사설 등을 영역했다. 2년 후 서울대학교에 입학해 한국어와 문학을 공부했고, 1965년 서울대학교에서 석사 학위를 받은 최초의 서양인이 되었다. 이어서 한국의 구전서사인 판소리에 관한 논문으로 하버드대학교에서 박사 학위를 받았다. 한국 현대문학 최초의 영문 선집 《한국에 귀 기울이기》(1973)를 편집했고 오영수의 단편집인 《착한 사람들》(1986)을 번역했으며 한국소설 선집 《유형의 땅: 현대 한국 소설》(1993)을 공역했다. 그 외에도 1994년 하버드대학교에서 그가 쓴 최초의 영문 판소리 연구서 《한국 민담 가수》가 나왔다. 하버드대학교에서 한국문학 전임강사와 여름학교 학장을 지낸 뒤 1995년 사망시까지 하와이대학교에서 한국문학을 가르쳤다.

Marshall R. Pihl saw Korea for the first time as a soldier in 1957, when he was assigned to the Public Information Office of the Korean Military Advisory Group in Seoul. Upon graduation from Harvard College in 1960, he returned to join the research department of the monthly journal *World of Thought* (Sasanggye), where he translated articles and editorials into English under the tutelage of the magazine's staff. Two years later, he entered Seoul National University to study Korean language and literature, emerging in 1965 as the first Westerner to have earned a master's degree there. Subsequent study led to the Harvard Ph.D. for a dissertation on the Korean oral narrative *p'ansori*. He edited one of the first English-language anthologies of contemporary Korean literature, *Listening to Korea* (Praeger, 1973); translated a collection of stories by Oh Yeongsu, *The Good People* (Heinemann Asia, 1986), co-translated the anthology *Land of Exile: Contemporary Korean Fiction* (M.E. Sharpe, 1993); and wrote the first English-language study of *p'ansori, The Korean Singer of Tales* (Harvard University Press, 1994). After serving as a Senior Lecturer on Korean Literature and Director of the Summer School at Harvard, he taught Korean Literature at the University of Hawai'i until his passing in 1995.

감수 **브루스 풀턴** Edited by Bruce Fulton

브루스 풀턴은 한국문학 작품을 다수 영역해서 영미권에 소개하고 있다. 『별사-한국 여성 소설가 단편집』『순례자의 노래-한국 여성의 새로운 글쓰기』『유형의 땅』(공역, Marshall R. Pihl)을 번역하였다. 가장 최근 번역한 작품으로는 오정희의 소설집 『불의 강 외 단편소설 선집』, 조정래의 장편소설 『오 하느님』이 있다. 브루스 풀턴은 『레디메이드 인생』(공역, 김종운), 『현대 한국 소설 선집』(공편, 권영민), 『촛농 날개-악타 코리아나 한국 단편 선집』 외 다수의 작품의 번역과 편집을 담당했다. 브루스 풀턴은 서울대학교 국어국문학과에서 박사 학위를 받고 캐나다의 브리티시컬럼비아 대학 민영빈 한국문학 기금 교수로 재직하고 있다. 다수의 번역문학기금과 번역문학상 등을 수상한 바 있다.

Bruce Fulton is the translator of numerous volumes of modern Korean fiction, including the award-winning women's anthologies *Words of Farewell: Stories by Korean Women Writers* (Seal Press, 1989) and *Wayfarer: New Writing by Korean Women* (Women in Translation, 1997), and, with Marshall R. Pihl, *Land of Exile: Contemporary Korean Fiction*, rev. and exp. ed. (M.E. Sharpe, 2007). Their most recent translations are *River of Fire and Other Stories* by O Chŏng-hŭi (Columbia University Press, 2012), and *How in Heaven's Name: A Novel of World War II* by Cho Chŏngnae (MerwinAsia, 2012). Bruce Fulton is co-translator (with Kim Chong-un) of *A Ready-Made Life: Early Masters of Modern Korean Fiction* (University of Hawai'i Press, 1998), co-editor (with Kwon Young-min) of *Modern Korean Fiction: An Anthology* (Columbia University Press, 2005), and editor of *Waxen Wings: The* Acta Koreana *Anthology of Short Fiction From Korea* (Koryo Press, 2011). The Fultons have received several awards and fellowships for their translations, including a National Endowment for the Arts Translation Fellowship, the first ever given for a translation from the Korean, and a residency at the Banff International Literary Translation Centre, the first ever awarded for translators from any Asian language. Bruce Fulton is the inaugural holder of the Young-Bin Min Chair in Korean Literature and Literary Translation, Department of Asian Studies, University of British Columbia.

바이링궐 에디션 한국 대표 소설 100

갯마을

2015년 1월 9일 초판 1쇄 발행

지은이 오영수 | 옮긴이 마샬 필 | 펴낸이 김재범
감수 브루스 풀턴 | 기획위원 정은경, 전성태, 이경재
편집 정수인, 이은혜, 김형욱, 유단비 | 관리 박신영
펴낸곳 (주)아시아 | 출판등록 2006년 1월 2일 제406-2006-000004호
주소 서울특별시 동작구 서달로 161-1(흑석동 100-16)
전화 02.821.5055 | 팩스 02.821.5057 | 홈페이지 www.bookasia.org
ISBN 979-11-5662-067-9 (set) | 979-11-5662-077-8 (04810)
값은 뒤표지에 있습니다.

Bi-lingual Edition Modern Korean Literature 100

Seaside Village

Written by Oh Yeongsu | **Translated by** Marshall R. Pihl
Published by Asia Publishers | 161-1, Seodal-ro, Dongjak-gu, Seoul, Korea
Homepage Address www.bookasia.org | **Tel**. (822).821.5055 | **Fax**. (822).821.5057
First published in Korea by Asia Publishers 2015
ISBN 979-11-5662-067-9 (set) | 979-11-5662-077-8 (04810)

바이링궐 에디션 한국 대표 소설

한국문학의 가장 중요하고 첨예한 문제의식을 가진 작가들의 대표작을 주제별로 선정!
하버드 한국학 연구원 및 세계 각국의 한국문학 전문 번역진이 참여한 번역 시리즈!
미국 하버드대학교와 컬럼비아대학교 동아시아학과, 캐나다 브리티시컬럼비아대학교 아시아
학과 등 해외 대학에서 교재로 채택!